W9-BDE-565

# SAY "AHHH!"
## Dora Goes to the Doctor

by Phoebe Beinstein
illustrated by A&J Studios

SCHOLASTIC INC.
New York  Toronto  London  Auckland  Sydney
Mexico City  New Delhi  Hong Kong  Buenos Aires

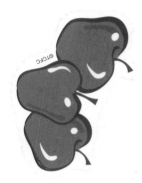

Based on the TV series *Dora the Explorer*® as seen on Nick Jr.®
No part of this publication may be reproduced, stored in a retrieval system, or transmitted in any
form or by any means, electronic, mechanical, photocopying, recording, or otherwise, without
written permission of the publisher. For information regarding permission, write to
Simon Spotlight, an imprint of Simon & Schuster Children's Publishing Division,
1230 Avenue of the Americas, New York, NY 10020.

ISBN-13: 978-0-545-07603-6
ISBN-10: 0-545-07603-X

Copyright © 2008 by Viacom International Inc. All rights reserved. Published by Scholastic Inc.,
557 Broadway, New York, NY 10012, by arrangement with Simon Spotlight, an imprint of
Simon & Schuster Children's Publishing Division. NICK JR., *Dora the Explorer*, and all related titles,
logos, and characters are registered trademarks of Viacom International Inc. SCHOLASTIC and
associated logos are trademarks and/or registered trademarks of Scholastic Inc.

12 11 10 9 8 7 6 5 4 3 2 1                                         8 9 10 11 12 13/0

Printed in the U.S.A.

First Scholastic printing, November 2008

*¡Hola! Soy* Dora. Today my *mami* is taking me for a checkup at the doctor. Will you come with me? Great! *¡Vámonos!*

First we have to find the examination room. Then the doctor will give me my checkup. Who do we ask for help when we don't know which way to go? Yeah, Map!

Map says first we have to go to the bus stop to take the number four bus which will take us to the doctor's office. Then we go into the waiting room where the nurse will call us into the examination room for my checkup.

Here we are at the bus stop. There are three buses coming. Do you see the number four bus? That's the one that will take us to the doctor's office.

There it is! *¡Número cuatro!* Number four! *¡Vámonos!* Let's go on the bus!

**Doctor's Office**

Press the buzzer, *por favor.*

The bus took us to the doctor's office, but the door to the waiting room is closed. The sign says press the buzzer. Will you help me press the buzzer? Press it! *Buzz! Buzz!*

Nurse Pilar is opening the door to the waiting room!

Nurse Pilar says that Dr. Lopez will be ready for us in a few minutes. There are lots of books and toys in the waiting room. Look at the puzzle on the floor! It's a picture of the human body. The heart is missing. Will you help me find it? *¡Gracias!*

*Mami* said that Nurse Pilar just called my name. That means we can go into the examination room for my checkup!

The first thing Nurse Pilar does is weigh and measure me to see how much I've grown. Wow, I've grown a lot since my last checkup. Do you know how tall you are and how much you weigh? Then she takes my temperature by putting a thermometer in my mouth. Nurse Pilar says my temperature is just right!

Now it's time for Dr. Lopez to come in and examine me. First she wants to listen to my heart with her stethoscope. She even lets me listen! It goes *lub, dub, lub, dub.* What does your heart sound like?

The next tool Dr. Lopez needs is a little hammer to test my reflexes. Do you see something that looks like a little hammer?

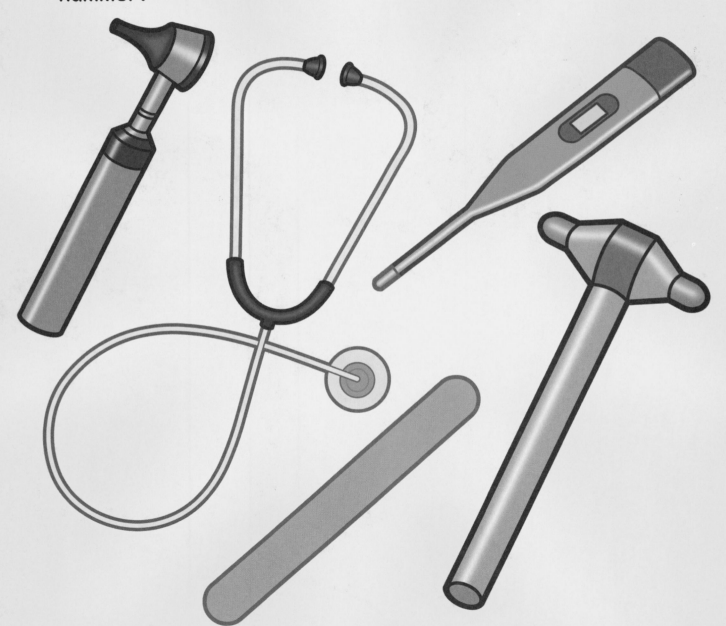

Yes, here it is! Dr. Lopez taps both my knees and makes them jump all by themselves.

Dr. Lopez asks me to open my mouth wide and make an "ahhh" sound so she can look at my throat. Make an "ahhh" sound with me. Say "Ahhh!"

She takes a little stick called a tongue depressor and gently presses on my tongue so she can see my throat. It looks like a frozen ice-pop stick!

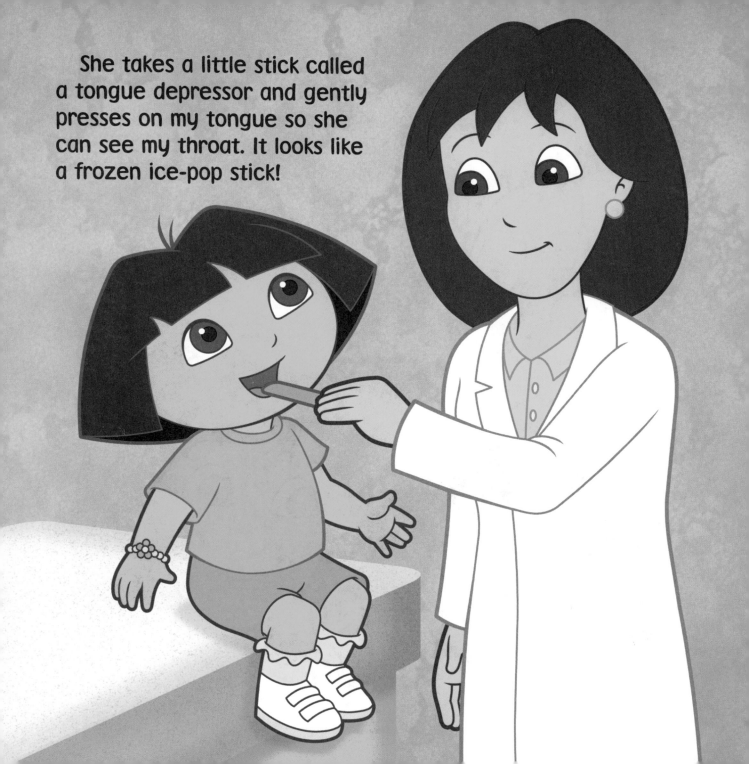

Her next tool is something called an otoscope. It has a little light on it to help her see into my eyes and ears and nose.

The last thing Dr. Lopez does is feel my tummy. She presses it a little bit all around. That tickles!

My checkup is all done. Dr. Lopez used all sorts of interesting instruments to make sure I'm healthy. And I am healthy! *¡Tengo salud!*

Now I get to choose a toy from the toy box for being such a good patient. I see a pink heart ring at the bottom. Will you help me reach it? Reach with your arm! Good reaching!

*Mami* says I was very brave at my checkup. She says you were too. I couldn't have done it without your help. *¡Gracias!*